Flore

a short story

With bonus story, Love Unlocked

ADRIA J. CIMINO

velvet morning
press

Published by Velvet Morning Press

ISBN-13: 978-0692437322
ISBN-10: 0692437320

Cover design by Ellen Meyer and Vicki Lesage
Author photo by Didier Quémener

Discover more by

BEST-SELLING AUTHOR

ADRIA J. CIMINO

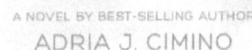

Flore

Apolline had been coming to the Café de Flore with her mother and grandmother just about every Wednesday afternoon since she was six. They lived practically around the corner, on the rue Bonaparte, which stretched from the Jardin de Luxembourg to the Seine. Apolline and her parents owned the top floor, and her grandmother the first floor of the same building.

The Flore routine had not changed much in ten years. The women would order tea and catch up on the happenings of the past week. They never sat on the terrace with the tourists. Their usual table was upstairs in the tiny room that was quiet at the teatime hour.

Apolline would order hot chocolate or cool fruit juice depending on the season, then doodle in her notepad or daydream. She would answer questions about school whenever her companions addressed her and follow them out the door when they were ready to leave.

But this time, Apolline broke the routine.

They were already halfway home when Apolline stopped suddenly. The two women, grandmother leaning on mother's arm for support, almost crashed into her.

"Apolline!"

"I'm sorry." She felt her face grow hot. "I forgot my notebook. I have to go back…"

Her mother rolled her eyes.

"You promised Professor Jacob that you would try to be more responsible, that you would come back down to earth and pay attention to the world around you."

Professor Jacob was Apolline's voice teacher, whose goal was to prep her for the conservatory. He and her mother—and everyone else for that matter—didn't understand that she *did* pay attention. When something interested her. And something at Flore had interested her, but she hadn't dared to share with her mother or grandmother.

Now as she nodded and turned around on her All Star-clad feet, she realized she didn't care what anyone thought or said at the moment. She wanted to return to the scene at Flore. She clutched her bag—an old Vuitton her mother had replaced with a newer version—and felt for the notebook that actually was nestled in its depths. She would need it after all. She always needed her notebook when something piqued her interest.

Apolline hardly saw or heard the crowd occupying every terrace table in the late spring sunshine. She took the steps two at a time and exhaled in relief as she discovered those she had wanted to see again were still there. And no one else.

She sat at the table she had occupied only minutes earlier, ordered a soda that would probably rot her teeth (according to her mother) and slid her trusty notebook out of her bag. In her looping teenage handwriting, she described the scene and hummed under her breath. Use of her singing voice in some way always calmed her.

The woman was still posing for photographs. She wasn't a model, but she was just as striking; tall and slender with large wide-set eyes. She had changed clothing a few times, unglamorously in the restroom about two steps from Apolline's table. With a laugh, she now pushed apart the saloon-style doors and emerged in a flaming orange dress that matched her hair and would surely stop traffic. Then her hand was on Apolline's arm.

"Darling, would you mind zipping the back?"

Apolline bit her lip and felt her heart flip flop. Because she *recognized* this woman. The singer of an underground band Apolline loved. She owned every album, sang every song. Of course not anywhere near the conservatory or within earshot of her parents. Both classical musicians, they turned up their noses at this sort of thing. Some classical musicians appreciated the underground stuff—Apolline even knew a few—but not her parents.

The singer, known simply as Lou, had spoken to her. And here Apolline was, frozen to the spot.

Lou's smile widened.

"I know you know who I am… and it's not a big deal being me. It's actually pretty ordinary. I mean, look, changing in the bathroom on the shoot for your album cover? Doesn't get better than that." She laughed again, and Apolline realized she was laughing too, and then zipping up the dress as if it was pretty ordinary.

The waiter arrived with Apolline's drink, popped the cap and poured until the froth bubbled right to the rim. It was an art that all café waiters had mastered.

"Ooh, can you bring me one of those too?" Lou asked.

The waiter nodded and disappeared. Parisian waiters were never impressed by celebrities. Maintaining a poker face was another art they had mastered.

Apolline was back in her seat, singing a hushed song to herself.

"C'mon Lou, hurry up," one of the photographers

called out. "Let's wrap this up."

"I'm all for it!" Then she turned back to Apolline. "Will you hang out for a bit? Have a drink with me?"

Apolline's heart flip flopped again and she felt her face turn hot. Suddenly, her voice—even the ever-present singing voice—disappeared.

So she nodded, her long brown ponytail bobbing up and down. It didn't matter that her mother was expecting her home momentarily. She slid her cell phone out of her bag and quickly typed a text message. She had run into her friend Charlotte and would hang around here with her for a while. Then she turned back to the action. She watched the final snapshots, listened to the playful banter between the singer and the photographer, and jotted words onto a page. To anchor this experience in her mind, forever.

What to say to a woman like Lou? *I'm a Left Bank kid who studies for the conservatory, wears my mother's designer hand-me-downs and rarely comes to this place by myself. But I'd rather sing in a band and forget about everything else.* No, that wasn't exactly interesting conversation. Wouldn't a wannabe say that? Yes. Apolline did not want to be a wannabe.

Apolline's phone buzzed, and she glanced at the message. *OK, but keep it short. Remember we have concert tickets tonight.* That's right… She had completely forgotten.

The waiter delivered Lou's soda as she sat down facing Apolline.

"You're a student at the conservatory?"

Apolline looked at her quizzically. She wasn't, yet the conservatory pretty much consumed her daily life anyway.

"You have a beautiful, trained voice, so I assumed…" Lou took a sip of her drink and waved to the photographer and his assistant as they lugged their equipment down the stairs.

Apolline blushed again. She hated the translucent

complexion that revealed every trace of embarrassment.

"I was singing to myself, it's sort of a habit because it's calm and soothing. I mean I've done it since I was little." Her words tumbled out in a jumble. "I do take voice, with the idea of going to the conservatory, but I don't really know if I want to go. Since my parents did, and are successful musicians, they see it as the only way."

"I went to the conservatory," Lou murmured.

"I didn't know... I mean, I never read those fan magazines. I just buy the music I like and don't bother much with the gossipy stuff."

Lou laughed and rubbed Apolline's arm as if they were old friends.

"Did you like the conservatory? Did you ever want to go for a classical career?"

"Yes, and no. There isn't only one outlet for talent. You can go to the conservatory, learn and then take your career in any direction you'd like."

Relief filled Apolline's heart. What had scared her so was the idea of this future, set in stone with no room for anything a bit whimsical. Her parents had repeated the goal over and over since she was a toddler.

"You've been sheltered, haven't you?" Lou said. "So was I."

Apolline bit her lip and glanced down at her lap, where her French-manicured nails toyed with the strap of her handbag.

"Why did you sit down here with me? I'm sure you've got better things to do."

"Because I heard your voice. And it reminded me of my own a few years ago."

Apolline's eyes widened.

"I don't know what to say.... Thanks... That's a real honor."

"I have a gig tonight at a small bar in the Marais."

"I know. I read about it."

"Do you want to sing with me?"

"Seriously?" Apolline nearly jumped out of her seat. And then her phone was ringing, her mother's name flashing on the screen.

"Just a sec," she whispered as she took the call. "I can't go to the concert... I know, I'm sorry, Mother. Uh, yeah, I'll be... studying with Charlotte. I forgot about an oral presentation we have to do tomorrow... OK, I know..."

"I won't tell you that you shouldn't be lying," Lou said with a shrug. "Sometimes, you have to get through somehow."

She glanced at the clock and rose from her seat.

"So you're coming?"

Apolline nodded and hastily gathered up her belongings.

Together, they dropped some coins on the table and hurried down the stairs into the early evening sunlight that threw their shadows across the sidewalk. In seconds, they were lost in the crowd.

Love Unlocked

Summer 2014

My flyers littered the bridge that I only wanted to protect. I chased after them as they fluttered out of careless hands and danced with the wind. For the better part of a week, I had stood on the Pont des Arts in front of the massive load of padlocks weighing down its frail skeleton.

"Do you know that when you attach one of those locks to the bridge, you're violating it? Read this, and you'll understand." But not many people wanted to understand. They didn't want to read my carefully prepared document detailing the structural and environmental damage caused by the locks. They were only interested in writing their names on locks and fastening them to the bridge's railings to attach their love story to the story of Paris.

In the best scenario, my audience had ignored me. In the worst, they had doused me with water and told me to go fuck myself. My gentle tactics clearly hadn't worked.

So after days of putting up with verbal abuse, it was time to be bold. I returned to the bridge at dusk and attached myself to it with my bicycle chain. A few people giggled, and others looked shocked. But, in all the hours I had spent on that bridge, this was the first time no one dared to fasten a lock... or even approach the railing.

Except one person. I saw him out of the corner of my eye. By now, night had fallen and my tired eyes scanned the pages of a classic I promised myself I would read before classes started in the fall. He seemed to be looking for something amid the layers of locks, and he was so absorbed in his search that he stepped on my foot. My toe now seemed as bright as the chipped, red nail polish I should have removed days ago.

"Excuse me!" he exclaimed as I let out a cry. "I didn't see you there."

"Forget it. I'm fine. What are you doing anyway, fiddling around there over my head?"

"Looking for a lock."

"Are you kidding? Do you actually think you're going to find some old lock in that mess of metal?"

"I think I remember where we put it..."

I shook my head and gazed through the misty gas-lamp light illuminating the river. Upside-down images of buildings and trees cast dark spots along the edges. And then there were the locks. Dark chunks of ugly metal growing across the bridge like aggressive tumors.

"You're a part of this, then," I said.

He stopped and looked down at me. For the first time, I saw his face. Beautiful on one side, marred on the other by a jagged scar. Like the bridge. I lowered my gaze for an instant. Enough time to mask the surprise.

"It's not like I put up every lock on this bridge!" he said. "You don't have to be so accusatory. You make it sound as if I'm in a conspiracy against mankind or something!"

"Fuck you… and all of you who hide behind everyone else! It's easy to say you weren't the first and to follow the crowd. That way, no one takes responsibility. Instead, you get defensive and then yell at the person who says what you don't want to hear. I know. I've seen that kind of shit all week."

"You've been here all week?"

"Chained, no. Unchained, yes. Chained worked better than unchained."

He lowered himself to the ground beside me, continuing his search and talking at the same time.

"How long are you going to stay here? Chained, I mean…"

"Well, I guess I'll eventually have to pee or take a shower. I didn't plan it out… I just needed to make this statement, to do something."

"Found it." His words were filled with both satisfaction and regret.

"OK, you found your lock. Now what? Are you going to, like, take a picture with it or kiss it? I discourage the kissing. Too many hands have touched those locks."

He smirked, yet his eyes, now nearer to me, seemed sad. They looked almost golden in the dimness.

"I'm unlocking it." He pulled a small key out of the pocket of his jeans, released the lock and tossed it into the trash can a few feet away.

"Why did you do that?"

"Our story is over. We broke up today."

"You only wanted to get rid of your lock because the relationship is over? Typical. You're not doing this because you care about the bridge or our environment."

"Typical of what? Of everyone except you? Of everyone who cares more about relationships and people than inanimate objects and vague ideas? You're a strange girl… uh… I don't know your name…"

I froze. I didn't need to have my personal life

dissected by some stranger. Did I really want to tell him that I was an ordinary girl who grew up in a farmhouse an hour from the city? Did I want to say that, there, watching my grandfather work, I learned to appreciate well-built structures and natural resources? And did I want him to know that in spite of the poor outcome of my recent dates, I cared about relationships probably as much as anyone else? No, no and no.

And then, before I could decide whether to snap back or not snap back, two sets of heavy black shoes settled nearly toe-to-toe with my flip flops. I looked up and straight into the faces of the police officers.

Then came the list of questions I should have expected, should have been ready to answer. Instead, I had been so focused on making a statement that I hadn't thought of the consequences. And that is how I found myself being carted off to the police station just before midnight. The young man I had been speaking with was no longer in sight.

I sat under the neon lights for I don't know how long. The outside of the station might have looked like the entrance to a dungeon centuries ago, but the inside was typical of a bland 1970s office with brown linoleum floors and stark white walls.

At least I had my book, but I kept reading the same passages over and over because I couldn't concentrate. Behind my poker face and nonchalant attitude, I was quaking with fear. It's not like I was used to being arrested. The most illegal thing I'd ever done was smoke a joint at my best friend's birthday party last year. This was decidedly new territory for me.

Finally, one of the officers I saw earlier called me into her office. I gave her the basics. Name? Anna Citron. Yes, I know it's funny that my last name means "lemon" in French. Age? 19. Yes, I know I'm lucky that I'm not a minor, and you don't have to embarrass me by calling my parents or guardians about this. Address? Rue Cardinal Lemoine. And yes, I know that Hemingway once lived on that street. But I live in a different building, and I'm not a writer. Just a literature student and I'm not sure what I'm going to do when I graduate. What the hell were you doing, Ms. Citron? Protecting the bridge, which is more than any of you have been able to do.

The police officer sighed, shook her head and leaned across the table toward me.

"Look, we could have you spend the night here. We could make a big deal out of it. But considering it's a first offense, if you can control the attitude, we can go easy."

I nodded, not quite sure what I was agreeing to, yet it didn't seem I had much of a choice.

"First of all, Ms. Citron, we don't want to see you chaining yourself to bridges again. This will be on your record. If you want more control over the law, go into politics. Now, let me see what I can do about the fine…"

"Fine?" I raised my eyebrows and thought about my meager budget.

She retreated into a back room, giving me plenty of time to worry and do mental calculations that in many cases involved me skipping meals and hocking a few pieces of inexpensive jewelry.

After another hour under the neons, I was a free woman. Thanks to some stranger who convinced them not only to let me go, but to waive the fine. I recognized him, half beauty, half beast, waiting in the lobby. His name was Justin.

"Thanks," I mumbled. "How did you swing that one?"

We were back on the street now, walking in the direction of the Seine.

"My motorcycle accident happened right around the corner… I got to know a few of the officers over there pretty well."

"The scar?"

"Yeah, along my arm and down the leg too."

"When did it happen?"

"Two years ago, on my way to pick up Pauline."

"The girl you just broke up with?"

"She broke up with me."

"Well, too bad for her!"

"That's nice of you, but I doubt she sees it that way. I think, for a long while, she felt guilty about my accident and the injuries... and a relationship can't be built on guilt."

"It was wrong of you to say that I care more about inanimate objects!" I snapped at him suddenly. "If I did, I wouldn't be feeling sad for you right now. I just so happen to care about people and the environment."

"Wanna sit down?" he asked.

I sat on Justin's good side, seeing the smoothness of one cheek. We dangled our legs over the edge of the riverbank. From afar, we heard laughter, crying and conversations. The sounds of a city that never sleeps.

"Why did you get me out of there, anyway?"

"I was curious."

"About what?"

"You. A girl who would chain herself to a bridge..."

"You thought I was a freak."

"Initially. But then I changed my mind. So what's your story?"

"If you think I hate the idea of romance or resent those supposedly happy couples sealing their love through metal, you're dead wrong." My snappy voice was back.

"I'm not thinking anything in particular..."

"Romance is something completely different. But that's another subject. The point is, I walked along the Pont des Arts so many times a few years ago, before the locks disfigured it. My last photo with my grandma was on that bridge. She pretty much raised me, out in the countryside… She would take me to the city a lot during the summer. I guess it's hard to see things change, and to accept that, when all you want is for things to go back to the way they used to be."

Strangely, I didn't feel the discomfort that usually would have arisen after such a declaration. Instead, I felt almost a sense of peace.

Justin's hand touched mine on the cool stone. I didn't move away. I caught his eye and smiled for the first time since we met. Slowly, the sky had been transforming itself from dark to light, from monochrome to multicolored.

"Do you think you'll do it again?" Justin asked.

"You mean chain myself to the bridge?"

He nodded.

"Not alone."

Justin smiled at me and shook his head. And then the two of us walked toward the sunrise.

About the Author

Adria J. Cimino is an author of contemporary literary fiction and a partner in the boutique publishing house Velvet Morning Press. She lives in Paris with her husband, daughter and son.

To follow Adria's latest adventures in Paris or learn about her upcoming books and writing projects, visit AdriaJCimino.com.

Adria's other books include:

A Perfumer's Secret: The quest for a stolen perfume formula awakens passion, rivalry and family secrets in the fragrant flower fields of the South of France.

Paris, Rue des Martyrs, a novel that paints an intriguing picture of the intertwining relationships of four strangers in Paris.

Before Paris, a short prequel to *Paris, Rue des Martyrs*.

Close to Destiny, a magical realism novel that explores the role of destiny in life.

Paris Jungle: What does Wanda Julienne, recently back to the corporate world after maternity leave, do when faced with a glass ceiling? Fight back.

That's Paris, an anthology of fiction and nonfiction stories about living, loving and surviving in the City of Light.

Legacy, an anthology that asks the question: What will you leave behind?

Read on for a sneak peek of *Paris, Rue des Martyrs*...

Paris

RUE DES MARTYRS

A NOVEL BY BEST-SELLING AUTHOR

ADRIA J. CIMINO

Chapter 1

Rafael

Rafael Mendez arrived like a thief in the night at 120 Rue des Martyrs. He ran all the way from the train station, where he had left one small, ragtag suitcase in a rented locker. His sneakers slapped noisily along the cobblestones, then pavement, in time with his own tears and the rain falling from a grim Parisian sky.

It was as if each minute lost counted for everything in his 23-year-old life. He pushed past umbrellas that seemed to tango as they bobbed against one another, old men who chatted with no one in particular, couples laughing, and a few sidewalk café tables left behind to weather the storm.

He was nearly blind to this first vision of the city, and only looked up now and again at the street signs to reassure himself that—yes—he hadn't lost the Rue des Martyrs. And then he stopped. He pushed wet strands of long, black hair back from his face, wiped away the silly tears of that odd combination of desperation and excitement, and sank down onto a bench facing the address he had imagined all of his life in Colombia.

Now, as the rain soaked through his jeans and his gaze traveled across the street to the only lighted apartment in building 120, his mind returned home. That's where his quest began, after all. In Bogotá.

๛

As a child, he would play with the emeralds. That was his first memory. Not mother. Not father. Emeralds. Because that was how his life began. His father never wanted to tell Rafael that the French jewelry designer gave birth to him on a trip for those precious stones. He only said it once—grimly—shaking his head and staring at the dark sand under their feet. Rafael remembered looking up at him with widened 10-year-old eyes as they plodded along the dusty trail to where his father would buy the stones. It was Rafael's first trip there with his father, and in the young boy's mind, it became a sacred place.

But he couldn't think of that story right now or those fucking emeralds. It was over. He had to erase every memory from his mind, the images that haunted him at night.

The one remaining light in 120 snapped off, leaving the building in darkness. It would be too late. He was wasting time. His heart raced as he crossed the street between the cars that kicked up muddy water onto his jeans. He ignored the honking horns. He wanted to move forward, and all at once he wanted to travel back. Rafael was frightened. Afraid of what he might learn or might not learn. Never be afraid, his father had hissed into his ear on that first trip for emeralds.

Before he could let his worries swallow him up with one great gulp, he pounded his fist on the heavy, brown-lacquered door that like a clamshell closed the apartments to the world. Nothing. The sound of his fist against the wood reverberated through his entire body, but no one responded. He scolded himself for his own impatience. How could he possibly have expected someone to answer that door at 11 o'clock on a Thursday night? He placed his hand softly against the handle and sighed, knowing he should leave, yet not able to abandon the glimmer of hope that his problems would be resolved in a matter of hours.

The door creaked open suddenly, and he jumped back.

"There's no need to be startled, you know. When you knock on a door like a maniac, you should expect it to open."

A wispy redhead slipped through the doorway and onto the sidewalk. She gave him a crooked grin, lit a cigarette and leaned against the cool brick.

"So," she said, blowing smoke to the sky, "who do you want to see that badly?"

Something about the young woman struck him. She wasn't beautiful, with her almost pasty complexion and skinny figure in oversized jeans, but she had an assertive air about her that was much more impressive.

"It must be pretty serious," she continued, taking a drag. "Why don't we talk about it?"

"Do you know a woman named Carmen?" Rafael asked, his voice shaking.

"No."

"Someone named Carmen lives or lived here…" he said, his words trailing off. He felt ridiculous and unprepared as he faced such inquisitive eyes.

"A lot of people have been around here," she said. "I need specifics."

"That's the problem. I don't have any."

"What have you come here for anyway?"

"Answers."

She flicked her half-smoked cigarette into the gutter and with green eyes paler than any emerald gazed up to the sky.

"What are your questions?"

A window flew open from above and a woman's voice called out: "Laurel? Laurel…"

The person who had to be Laurel pulled Rafael against her and ducked into the shadows. She grinned mischievously.

"I've got to run."

His heart skipped a beat as her hair brushed against his cheek. But he kept any flicker of sentiment in check. He didn't have time for distractions.

"Meet me back here tomorrow—same hour," Laurel whispered. "I'll see what I can find out. I have some connections…" And then she slipped away from him and into the night.

Find out what happens next… buy *Paris, Rue des Martyrs* today!

Discover more by

BEST-SELLING AUTHOR

ADRIA J. CIMINO

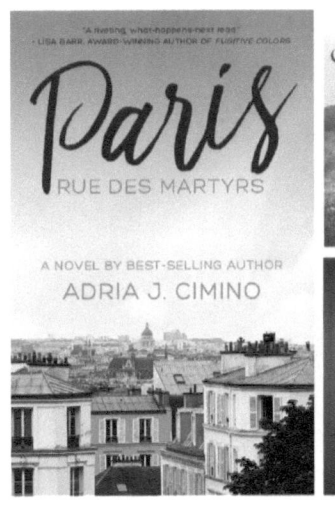